Tiger Heat

Books by Sigmund Brouwer

SPORTS MYSTERY SERIES

#1 *Maverick Mania*

#2 *Tiger Heat*

#3 *Cobra Threat* (available 8/98)

#4 *Titan Clash* (available 10/98)

LIGHTNING ON ICE SERIES

#1 *Rebel Glory*

#2 *All-Star Pride*

#3 *Thunderbird Spirit*

#4 *Winter Hawk Star*

#5 *Blazer Drive*

#6 *Chief Honor*

SHORT CUTS SERIES

#1 *Snowboarding to the Extreme . . . Rippin'*

#2 *Mountain Biking to the Extreme . . . Cliff Dive*

#3 *Skydiving to the Extreme . . . 'Chute Roll*

#4 *Scuba Diving to the Extreme . . . Off the Wall*

CYBERQUEST SERIES

#1 *Pharaoh's Tomb*

#2 *Knight's Honor*

#3 *Pirate's Cross*

#4 *Outlaw's Gold*

#5 *Soldier's Aim*

#6 *Galilee Man*

THE ACCIDENTAL DETECTIVES MYSTERY SERIES

WINDS OF LIGHT MEDIEVAL ADVENTURES

Tiger Heat

SIGMUND BROUWER

Thomas Nelson, Inc.

Nashville

TIGER HEAT

Published in Nashville, Tennessee, by Tommy Nelson™,
a division of Thomas Nelson, Inc.

Executive Editor: Laura Minchew; Managing Editor: Beverly Phillips.
Cover Photo: S. Chenn / Westlight

Library of Congress Cataloging-in-Publication Data

Brouwer, Sigmund, 1959–
    Tiger heat / Sigmund Brouwer.
        p. cm.—(Sports mystery series)
        Summary: A group of teenagers, calling themselves the Sewer
Rats, play a game of paintball war in the city sewer tunnels that
turns deadly serious.
    ISBN 0-8499-5814-8
    [1. Paintball (Game)—Fiction. 2. Christian life—Fiction.]
I. Title. II. Series: Brouwer, Sigmund, 1959–   Sports mystery
series.
PZ7.B79984Ti 1998
[Fic]—dc21

                                                    98-14584
                                                       CIP
                                                        AC

Printed in the United States of America
99 00 01 02 03 QPV 9 8 7 6 5 4 3 2

To Janet Reed—
you're wonderful.

One

Here it is, Miss Winkle, the whole story about how I ended up in the hospital.

I sure hope you haven't forgotten our deal. You know I've missed a lot of school and have a ton of make-up work to do. You agreed that you'd give me a passing grade for my missed time if I made a writing assignment out of this. So I guess you get the details on how a church kid like me got into trouble with a bunch of kids called the Sewer Rats.

I remember you once said that good writing isn't about getting hung up on spelling and punctuation rules. You said it's about making pictures with words. And about getting better with practice, just like in sports. You said good writers are the ones who tell their stories as honestly as they can.

I figure that's why you have me filling up this note-book—so I can learn both how to write better and how to be honest.

You never told me, though, that it would be so hard to decide where to start. I mean—and this is being honest—part of this happened because I was mad at my parents. They made me play baseball with a bunch of kids everyone called losers. And I didn't like being forced to believe in what my parents believe in. I mean, a person should have a choice in that, right? And a little bit of it happened because I didn't want anyone to find out how often I get afraid. But I'm not sure I want to start with all of that.

Instead, I'm going to do what you taught our class about writing. It might surprise you to find out I was actually paying attention. I remember how you said it was important to start with the four corners of a story. *Who. When. Where. What.*

So here I go.

Who?

That's easy. Me, Jim McClosky. And my friends, Lisa Chambers and Micky Downs. Lisa and Micky called themselves the Sewer Rats before I met them. That's because of the paintball wars that happen in the tunnels beneath the streets. The Sewer Rats rule the sewers. I became a Sewer Rat later, after my folks forced me to hang out with Lisa and Micky on the baseball team.

More on us. I'm short and skinny and dark haired. When I get to choose, I almost always lose myself in a good science fiction book. Lisa Chambers is blond and pretty, with a sweet face and big eyes, like a china doll—but she's a lot tougher than she looks. Micky has light brown short hair, a square face, and square shoulders. His dad was a policeman who was killed on duty.

When did it begin?

Just after sundown on a Wednesday. I guess I should have been doing my homework instead of trying to fit in with the Sewer Rats, but like I said, I was mad at my folks.

Where did this story start?

Down at the park, where the ponds are. You know the place. Near the playground. Where all the ducks and geese hang out. There are two little platforms over the ponds for bands to perform on during the summer. Because of the rain we've had, the ponds are overflowing their banks, and the walkway between the platforms is kind of hard to get to. The ground around the ponds is pretty slimy and slippery, and it doesn't smell too good.

Of course, kids aren't supposed to be there after dark. There's a fence around the park to keep people out at night.

Which leads to the fourth corner of how you said we should start a story: *what* Micky and Lisa and I were doing hanging out near the duck ponds just after sundown on a Wednesday night.

We were watching from outside the fence. The new kid in class was picking his way between snoozing birds. Then he jumped from the muddy bank onto one of the platforms. He waved as he positioned himself at one end of the walkway between the platforms.

What he had to do next was almost like crossing a tightrope.

TWO

The three of us behind the fence leaned against it, so that it bent inward a bit with our weight. I had my fingers wrapped around the linked steel.

We were on the safe side of the fence. Joey Saylor, the new kid, was inside, where he wasn't supposed to be. He was about the length of a football field away from us, on the walkway above a smelly duck pond. He had ragged blond hair that almost reached his shoulders. He wore black jeans, a black T-shirt, and new Nikes.

As we watched, he climbed onto the metal railing of the walkway.

"I hope Joey doesn't wake all those ducks," Micky said. "They'll make enough noise to bring the security guard out of the building."

"He's stupid enough to get caught," Lisa said. Her voice was angry.

I half turned my head to look at her. *What had this guy ever done to her?*

Lisa saw me turn my head. "If I want to think he's stupid, I can," she told me. "And I can say it too. Do you have a problem with that?"

Lisa gets into trouble sometimes because of her quick temper. My dad says it's because she's not a happy person. He also says I should look past her temper to see her good side. He's always reminding me that I'm on the baseball team to be a positive role model.

"Nope," I answered Lisa. It was best to keep her good side on my side. "Joey might be stupid. But I'm not."

The frown on her face told me I shouldn't ask her why she disliked the new kid so much. But as far as I could see, all Joey had done was ask how he could join the Sewer Rats.

I thought it would happen the way I had joined. I'd had to prove myself in a paintball game in the sewer tunnels below the streets. Micky and Lisa wanted to know that I wasn't scared of the dark tunnels, that I could be a help to them in the wars.

But Lisa had told Joey that we Sewer Rats proved ourselves in a test at the duck ponds. This test was sneaking inside the fence and balancing on the railing above the slimy water and sleeping ducks.

"Stupid or not," Micky said, watching Joey carefully, "you've got to admit he's got guts."

Joey was in plain view on the walkway. The security guard could notice him any second. His arms were stretched wide as he balanced himself, taking one careful step at a time.

"Guts? I hope he gets caught," Lisa said. "Or, better yet, that he falls in."

I glanced at Lisa and wondered again what Joey had done to make her so mad. He'd only been at school a couple of days. He and his family had just moved to town.

I looked back at Joey.

He had made it halfway across, walking the railing like he was part of a tightrope act.

I looked at the brown slimy water in the pond below him. Brown slimy water with feathers floating in it. Brown slimy water where ducks did a lot more than just paddle. I wondered what would happen if a security guard caught him. I started to get a scared feeling in my stomach, like a ball of spiders wriggling around. The same scared feeling I get every time I go into the tunnels for a paintball war against another team.

Zantor, soldier of the galaxy, I thought silently. *The mighty warrior has removed all emotion as he watches a rookie soldier go up against the alien swamp.*

Mom and Dad have always told me that praying is a good way to deal with fear. But I have my own way. By making this a pretend world, I can make the ball of spiders stop wriggling in my stomach. That's what I do whenever I'm scared—anywhere. In school before a test. Facing down a wild pitcher in a baseball game. And in the dark tunnels beneath the streets. I pretend I am someone else.

You see, scared as I get in the tunnels, there is no way I can let Micky or Lisa know it. Ever. One, the Sewer Rats are my friends. Two, I need to prove to myself that I can always beat my fear. And three, I don't want a single person in the world to ever know I'm scared.

I stayed in my pretend world and kept watching the new kid.

Zantor smiles. The swamp test provides amusement for the galaxy soldier.

Finally, the spiders of fear in my stomach stopped wriggling.

Lisa stepped back from the fence. Sounds of rustling nylon and a zipper told me that she was opening her school backpack. She began to dig through it.

I didn't take my eyes off Joey to see what she was doing.

"What's that?" Micky asked Lisa a few seconds later.

"What's it look like?" she retorted. "A violin?"

Curious, I looked over. Lisa had an airhorn in her hands, the kind that uses pressurized air to make noise. Loud noise. I found out just how loud a second later as it almost shattered my eardrums.

Micky spun and shouted at her. "What are you—"

Lisa cut Micky off by blaring the airhorn again.

I saw Joey stagger a bit on the railing, like he had jumped at the sudden sound.

Lisa blared the airhorn in more short blasts.

Three things happened.

Ducks and geese woke up and added to the noise by quacking, honking, and flapping their wings.

Several people came running, including a big security guard.

And Joey saw the security guard and lost his balance. He dropped into the pond like a giant rock. Then he began to splash in the slimy water like crazy.

"Help!" Joey shouted. "I can't swim. Help! Help!"

He splashed and splashed, even though the pond was only a couple of feet deep.

As the ducks and geese started toward the pond to investigate, Lisa just giggled and giggled.

Three

About twenty-four hours later, I was afraid again. But this time I was afraid for me, not for someone else.

I stood at home plate. We already had two outs. We were up 8–7, top of the ninth inning. We had two runners on base. Micky was waiting at third. He had gotten on base with a walk and had run to third on Lisa's double. Lisa was watching me from second base.

If I could get a hit, I would drive in one run, maybe even two. One or two extra runs would really help as we went into the bottom of the ninth.

But I was probably the only person on the team who cared. Baseball is a great game. It has history and tradition. It takes skill and smart thinking. I even like to watch it when I'm not playing.

Micky and Lisa and the other Tigers might like baseball, but they weren't going to show it. Some of them were only on the team because a judge had ordered them to be. A court-approved after-school program was supposed to keep them out of trouble. The program at my parent's church was one of those approved by the court. And it included participating on a team in the city baseball league.

I almost wished I was like them. I almost wished I didn't care that our team was in last place. That way it wouldn't matter that I was afraid of getting hit by the ball.

Think about it. A fastball in the chin? No thanks. If I didn't care about the game, I could just let the pitches go past me and stay out of their way.

But I did care. And I didn't want anyone to know I was afraid of getting hit.

The pitcher reared back. He looked huge, with the straggly beginnings of a mustache. Kids in junior high shouldn't be big enough to even think about mustaches.

His arm snapped forward. The baseball hissed.

I squared up to lay down a bunt, just like Coach Martin had told me. I closed my eyes. The ball clunked against the bat. When I opened my eyes, I watched the ball dribble foul.

Behind me, cheers and groans came from the stands. Mainly parents, it wasn't a big crowd. And none of the parents belonged to Micky or Lisa or me. Micky's dad was dead, and his mom worked full time. Lisa's parents were divorced, and she lived with her mom, who was always too tired to come to her games. As for my mom and dad, they came when they could, but I have four sisters and a brother, so things are usually too crazy for them to get away. That suited me just fine. I didn't want them to watch me strike out, again.

The pitcher readied himself for the next pitch, kicking dirt and trying to look like a pro.

My insides tightened. Here came one more pitch to survive.

"Hey shorty," the catcher behind me said, "I hear you haven't had a hit in six games."

Catchers always say stuff like that to throw off batters.

"Actually seven," I shot back. "But you probably can't count that high."

That kept him quiet.

The next pitch hissed in like another snake of torment. I began to square up to bunt again, then thought better of it and jumped back. The ball almost brushed my shirt.

"He's got more like that," the catcher said with a sneer in his voice. "Quit crowding the plate."

I nearly laughed. I *never* crowd the plate. As much as I love baseball, I'm not willing to risk the pain of getting hit.

Still, I backed away a little as the catcher threw the ball back to the pitcher.

"One and one," the umpire called.

I took my stance again. I heard a voice above the cheers from the crowd.

"Jimmy! Jimmy! Jimmy! You get 'em Jimmy! Go, Jimmy, go!"

It was Coach Martin. Dressed in his usual sweats, he was a tall, skinny guy, just out of college. He flashed me his familiar grin. His short blond hair looked wild in the wind. "Go, Jimmy, go!"

When was Coach Martin going to learn that most of the team made fun of him behind his back for his cheering?

The third pitch came in like a meteor. I gave it a feeble poke that was not quite a swing and not quite a bunt. The ball popped off my bat and flew almost straight up.

The catcher threw off his mask, backed up, and caught the ball easily.

He gave me a smirk of triumph.

"That makes eight," I said before he could mouth off. "Eight games without a hit. That's the number that comes after seven. And before nine. Got it, rock brain?"

He stared at me, as if wondering whether he should say something. He must have remembered what kind of kids play for the Tigers because he kept his mouth shut. Most kids are afraid to mess with the Tigers.

The Tigers came about as part of a program that my parents' church runs. It's an outreach thing that's supposed to help troubled kids build character. The city league was glad to add another team. Most of the other teams come from the schools in the area.

So far, the Tigers hadn't learned much more than how to field grounders and swing at pitches. My parents had the idea that I could be a good influence on

14

some of the other kids who were here as part of their probation. So they had volunteered me. But the catcher didn't know that. Guess this is one time our team's bad reputation was a good thing.

Although I was afraid, I stared at the catcher until he looked away.

I didn't apologize to anyone for stranding two runners. I didn't apologize later when the other team scored two runs in the bottom of the ninth to beat us by one run.

After all, we were the Tigers. It wouldn't be cool if my teammates knew how much I cared.

Four

We three Sewer Rats met at a nearby 7-Eleven right after the game. We bought Cokes, then hung out in the parking lot with our bikes.

"It's like this," Micky said to Lisa, "maybe we should lay low for a while."

"We?" she asked, kicking at a chocolate bar wrapper on the ground.

"The Sewer Rats. Maybe we should hold off on Saturday's paintball war against the guys from Medford."

I wasn't surprised that we didn't spend a single second talking about the baseball game we had just lost. They didn't care, and I was getting used to their attitude.

"No way," she said. "Not a chance. We don't back away. We're Sewer Rats—not Sewer Chickens."

Her tone of voice didn't scare Micky like it did me.

"Look," he said. "Yesterday—"

"What about yesterday?" she asked. "Some stupid kid fell in a duck pond and had to get rescued by security. That's not our fault."

I shook my head at the memory. The guard had reached Joey without too much trouble, in spite of the ducks he'd had to dodge. After all, the water wasn't very deep. But they'd both had a tough time climbing out on the slippery, smelly bank. Once I knew Joey was safe, it was pretty funny to watch his feet shoot out from under him in the mud.

"Not our fault?" Micky said. "Who started with the airhorn?"

"Part of the test," she said. "He failed. That's no reason for us to chicken out of the paintball game on Saturday."

"But what I'm trying to say," Micky said, "is that because the security guard called the principal at the school, just about everyone knows Joey fell in the pond."

"Most people think it was funny," Lisa said. "Besides they don't know it was us."

Micky started to say something else, then looked up and shut his mouth. A man in a suit walked past us to go into the 7-Eleven. The man frowned at us, like we were doing something wrong by hanging out in front of the store.

"The teachers know about it too," Micky said after the man went into the store. "They don't think it's funny. Maybe we should lay low until everyone forgets about this."

"The teachers can't do anything to us," Lisa told

him, defiantly crossing her arms. "It was Joey who climbed over the fence, not us."

"But—" Micky tried. It was like trying to stop a hurricane.

"Besides, do you think I care what teachers think?" Lisa asked. "It's the Medford guys I care about. The Sewer Rats have never lost a paintball war, and we're not going to chicken out now."

"Hey," I said. I pointed down the street.

Joey headed toward us on his mountain bike. The wind blew his blond hair straight back.

"What's he doing here?" Lisa asked. "Who told him we were going to meet here?"

"I did," Micky answered.

"He's not a Sewer Rat!" Lisa was angry.

"After what he went through yesterday, he's part of us," Micky said, crossing his own arms. "He didn't say a word about us to that security guard or about why he was in the duck pond. He took full blame, and I bet it cost him plenty. If he's not in, I'm not in."

Lisa glared at Micky. Micky calmly stared straight into her eyes.

"Come on," I said. "You guys are friends. Think of all the times you've helped each other in the tunnels."

They kept staring at each other.

Joey pulled up, doing a brake slide as he stopped.

"Hey," he said.

I started to sniff the air. "Something smells."

"Very funny," Joey said, still grinning. "The pond muck washes out. Really."

He continued. "Of course, it took three bottles of shampoo to get clean."

I laughed and gave him a high-five.

"What's with those two?" Joey asked me.

Micky and Lisa were still staring at each other.

"Not much," I said. "Any second they're going to kiss and make up."

Finally, Lisa uncrossed her arms.

"Are we on for a paintball war with the Medford team on Saturday after the baseball game?" she asked Micky.

"Sure," he said after a couple of seconds. "With Joey, our new Sewer Rat?"

Lisa darted a dirty look at Joey. "I guess so."

Joey smiled at her.

That was pretty much the end of our meeting.

It wasn't until that night as I fell asleep that I began to wonder about something.

Because of Lisa's airhorn, Joey had fallen into the pond. Because of us, Joey had gotten into big trouble. Yet he had been friendly, as if nothing had happened to sabotage his initiation. He hadn't even mentioned the airhorn.

I couldn't figure it out.

Why wasn't Joey mad at us—especially Lisa?

 # *Five*

Saturday morning, as we warmed up for our game under sunshine and high wispy clouds, a police cruiser pulled up to the diamond.

Micky, at shortstop, fired a ball to me on first, like it didn't matter to him that the police had showed up. I caught the ball and threw a bad looper to Lisa at third base; it did matter to me. After all, Micky had told me what he'd done the night before.

The car door of the police cruiser slammed shut. I imagined the officer hitching his pants as he looked around the diamond. I didn't even glance at him, though. If we were lucky, he was just here to watch his kid play our team.

A few seconds later, I found out we weren't that lucky.

"Jim!" Coach Martin called. "Micky! Come here a second!"

I waited for Micky to join me from shortstop. Together, we shuffled our way to the dugout.

I felt all eyes on us. There wasn't a huge crowd in the bleachers, but suddenly it felt like there were hundreds of people staring at us.

Micky and I pretended it was no big deal to be called out by a big policeman. He put his hands on his hips as he glared down on us.

Any chitchat in the stands had stopped. All the Tigers on the field were watching us. Everyone on the other team was looking over at us. It seemed like time had stopped, like Micky and I were stuck in some sort of weird 3-D photograph.

Maybe Coach Martin noticed. Even though we still had five minutes of warm-up left, he whistled for the rest of the team to come in.

"Send your team out," he yelled at the other coach.

With all the chaos and noise that followed, time began to move around us again. It put the four of us into our own little world—me and Micky, tall Coach Martin in red Nike sweats, and the round-faced big policeman in uniform.

"Frankly, Officer," Coach Martin said. "I don't understand why you would choose this time and place to—"

"Look," the big man snapped. "Any other time and I wouldn't be able to find these punks. As soon as this game is over, they'll be gone like smoke, probably off to break into the house of some other family gone on vacation. The one I'm here about lost a television and a stereo." He looked pointedly at us. "But then you wouldn't know anything about that, would you?"

The Tigers had played fifteen games this season.

We'd lost most of them, and many of them badly. We'd been ripped by bad calls, shouted at by parents, and jeered by other players. During all that, few of the Tigers except for me had given much more effort than it took to run the bases. Yet not once had Coach Martin lost his calm smile.

In other words, most of the Tigers thought he was a pushover, a wimp. But the officer had barely finished speaking when I saw different.

"I expect you will apologize to these boys," Coach Martin said. He had not moved, but somehow he seemed taller and stronger. The peace in his eyes was replaced with a fire. "They deserve the same respect you would give any citizen."

"Apologize?" The big man snorted. "That will be the day. These brats—"

"These young men," Coach Martin interrupted with steel in his voice, "will answer any questions you ask, as long as you ask them politely. They will not be pre-judged or insulted. If you want to hide behind your badge and bully someone, at least pick on someone your own age and size."

The officer looked Coach Martin up and down for a long moment. Coach Martin did not back away. He stared right back. The officer's face got redder and redder.

"Bible-thumping do-gooder," the policeman mumbled at Coach Martin. In a stronger voice, he added, "Some day you'll see what a fool you are for trying to protect these kids. Oh, I know the theory, all right.

Have them report to you instead of a parole officer. Give them an activity and a chance to believe in themselves."

The officer spit on the ground. "What a load of garbage. These kids have lost most of their games. They don't care about baseball. All they believe in is what they can steal or destroy."

He looked at us. "I'll be heading to your parents' houses now. We'll see what they have to say about your whereabouts last night. Even if you weren't the ones who broke into the house in question, I'm sure you're guilty of something."

I did feel guilty. Although I hadn't done anything, I knew who had. Was keeping my mouth shut like being part of it? On the other hand, I wouldn't have become friends with Micky if my parents hadn't volunteered me for this baseball team. I would have preferred to play on the school team, a winning team.

The officer shook his head with a frown, speaking to Micky. "And you. Your father was a great policeman. A hero. If he were alive today, he would be so ashamed of what you turned out to be."

The muscles at the back of Micky's jaws made little balls. A sure sign he was about to start a fight. I stepped in front of him to keep him from rushing the officer.

"That is enough," Coach Martin said quietly. "It's time for you to leave."

"Leave?" the policeman said. "I'm just getting started."

"If these boys are suspects, they have legal rights,

which include the right to a lawyer," Coach Martin said. "If they are not suspects, they are only bound by respect to speak to you. And you, sir, do not deserve respect. That I can plainly see."

Wow.

Again, they stared at each other, eyeball-to-eyeball. The policeman was the first to break.

He turned away, stopped, and looked back at Coach Martin. "I don't care how many major-league ball teams wanted to draft you, mister. These kids deserve to spend time in reform school, and you won't be able to help them one bit. Stay in church where you belong and preach to the white-hairs who have nothing better to do than sit and listen to you."

Major-league ball? We all knew Coach Martin was a preacher in my parents' church. But who knew he was a major-league player?

The officer marched back to his car and slammed the door. He scattered gravel as he pulled away.

Coach Martin let out a long breath.

"Well," he said, "time to play ball."

I thought it was pretty cool that he didn't ask us if we knew who had broken into that house. Or maybe he was smarter than he looked and didn't want to force us to lie to him.

Six

A couple of our players had been close enough to overhear. By the middle of the second inning, everyone on the team knew what had happened during our chat with the officer.

I looked up and down the bench to see the whispers and disbelief. Disbelief that major-league teams had wanted to draft Coach Martin. And disbelief that he had taken our side against a policeman.

After all, the officer had been right in describing the team. Micky was here because he'd gotten into one too many fights. Lisa had been caught shoplifting. Someone else on the team had been caught riding in a stolen car. Only a couple of us had clean records. We were supposed to be role models, to be around if anyone had questions about the church—what we believed in and stuff.

That would have been okay, except that I sometimes wondered myself. And, of course, there was the

other reason I wasn't a good role model. In the beginning, I had been so mad about not having a chance to
play for a better team that I had decided to become
more like the Tigers.

Coach Martin had put up with us all season, even
though it was clear he was the only one who thought
we could be winners, on or off the field.

When baseball season ended, the outreach program
would offer different activities, depending on the
time of year: camping and canoeing, basketball.
Anything to keep the Tigers too busy to get in more
trouble.

It wasn't working of course. Most of the kids still
managed to get into trouble, just not during the time
we were supposed to report in for our practices and
games.

But Coach Martin still seemed to enjoy trying to
help the Tigers. He had never yelled at us, had never
preached at us, had never gotten mad at us for slack-
ing off in practices and games. Most of the kids
thought he was just a goody-two-shoes preacher and
didn't take him too seriously.

But now whispers kept flying up and down the
bench.

*He'd had major-league offers, and he'd never men-
tioned it to any of us?*

He'd stood up to an officer to protect the Tigers?

It gave us a whole new look at Coach Martin. He'd
fooled us with his baby-blue eyes and boyish face.

By the time we took the field for the third inning,

we were a whole new ball team. The Tigers were actually going to try.

We were down 3–0. Their best batter, a guy with wide shoulders and almost-black hair, stepped up to the plate. He grinned with confidence.

For a good reason.

Our chubby red-headed pitcher, whose real name is Luke Clemens, has a nickname: Rainbow. That's because his pitches are so slow, they drop like rainbows as they reach the plate.

Just before Rainbow threw his first pitch of the inning, Micky called his name and trotted toward him. They talked quietly for a few minutes. Rainbow nodded.

"Hey Coach," Rainbow called. "Can Micky pitch?"

"I don't know," Coach Martin called back. "Can he?"

Because of what he had done for us with the police, I forgave him his nerdy joke.

With his usual grin, Coach Martin nodded and waved, giving them the okay to switch positions.

But Rainbow didn't go to shortstop. He came my direction, to where I stood at first base.

"Micky wants you to go to shortstop," Rainbow said. "My arm's not good enough to throw anyone out."

Me? But shortstop has a lot of pressure. If a ball came my way, I might . . .

I saw Micky give me a thumb's-up.

I hid my fear.

The ambassador of the planet XVQuignum had sent an urgent request across the galaxy. Zantor was needed. Zantor never failed under pressure. Zantor . . .

"Sure," I said. "I'll play shortstop."

"And Micky said to play hard," Rainbow added. "He said it would be great to win this game."

We were still down by the end of seven innings, but only by one run. No surprise to me, Micky was a great pitcher. His fastball had plenty of pop. He was even able to throw a pretty good sinker. No matter how hard a player swung at his sinker, the ball would always drop into the dirt.

During those four innings as a rookie shortstop, I'd even handled a couple of medium-hop grounders. Medium-hops are the worst. The long-hops—the ones that bounce way out into the infield—are easy. You just keep your eye on the ball and watch it all the way into your glove. Short-hoppers are almost as easy. Get your body in the way, scoop the ball up, and hope it sticks in your glove. But medium-hoppers?

If Coach Martin hadn't spent hours hitting balls to us, I wouldn't have had a chance. You have to keep your head down and make quick moves with your hands without flinching the rest of your body.

As we all began to try harder, the practice sessions we thought we hadn't paid attention to began to pay off.

Lisa, playing second base, had turned a double play by diving for a fly ball, landing with it in her glove. Then she'd fired it from her knees to second where I was covering for her. We'd twice trapped runners between bases, running them back and forth until Lisa tagged them out. And none of our outfielders had dropped easy fly balls.

We were actually playing like a baseball team.

The score stayed 3–2 through the top of the ninth. I was the fourth batter in the bottom of the ninth. When I reached the plate, we only had one out, with Micky on second and Lisa on first.

I had a weird feeling at the plate. It took me a second to figure it out. Instead of my usual fear, I just wanted to get a hit.

I dug my feet in, bat ready on top of my shoulder.

"Heading to jail after the game?" the catcher asked me, figuring I was one of the Tigers sent here by a judge. The catcher hadn't spoken all game, I guess because until now he figured we'd be easy to beat.

"Yes, I am," I said. "To visit your mother."

I was pretty happy with that little remark—so happy that I didn't realize what was happening until it was too late.

The catcher had given the pitcher a sign to dust me with a fastball. It came in like a bazooka shell, aimed for my chin.

All I could do was fall out of the way. I landed on my bottom. A roar of laughter reached me from the stands.

I dusted myself off.

It didn't occur to me to charge the pitcher. Some

guys might have. It just made me so mad that I focused on slamming the next pitch out of the park.

It came in hot, just over the outside corner. Somehow I got my hips and arms and shoulders all into the bat and the ball at the same time.

The solid thunk of ball connecting with bat felt good on my hands. I watched the ball head up and away.

That was my hit?

I was still standing there in disbelief when Lisa came around from third.

"Hey, Einstein," she called out. "When it goes over the fence like that, it's called a home run. But you still have to run the bases."

I headed for first, my arms high in the air.

Seven

That Saturday afternoon, the Sewer Rats met in the tall trees at the edge of Bell Park.

We all wore backpacks that held our helmets. And we all carried guitar cases. Inside the cases were our paintball guns. Yes, guitar cases looked odd. But we knew people would never stop us to ask us about music practice. On the other hand, plenty of people would have had plenty of questions if we walked around with paintball guns over our shoulders.

And what we were doing, of course, was something we didn't want many people to ask about.

After all, we don't live in a big city. Haystown, built along the Grand River in Michigan, has maybe 40,000 people. It looks like an old-fashioned painting with a courthouse, town square, and buildings about a hundred years old. People here don't just mind their own business. They'll help people in trouble. They'll ask questions of kids on their way to Bell

Park. And they'll stop us if they think we're up to some kind of mischief.

The park has acres and acres of paths and big trees.

In the middle of the park, there's a drainage ditch that empties into the river. On the lower side of the big hill that slopes down toward Bell Park, a big culvert dumps into this ditch. The culvert is connected to the entire drainage system below the streets.

It's a big system, a whole maze of tunnels.

The main purpose of the tunnels is to collect water. When it rains, water runs into street gutters. These small streams reach grates and drop into the tunnels below the streets.

A one-hour rainstorm might not sound like much, but after a few minutes, there are thousands and thousands of these little streams on the streets, emptying into the tunnels.

It adds up. Fast. In fact, the main tunnel that drains into Bell Park can become a solid pipeline of fast-moving water as high as a person's waist pretty quickly.

That's why we never have paintball wars when it looks like it might rain. We don't want to take the chance of getting caught in a flood in the tunnels.

Today, though, looked like a great day. The wind was blowing, but there were no clouds. And it didn't matter that the wind was cold. In the tunnels, you only hear the wind when it blows through the grates above.

"Guys," Micky said as we began to walk along a path to the middle of the park. "Last night, Lisa and I decided we should use the mousetrap plan. We've heard these Medford guys think they're real commando types. So it only makes sense that we play the waiting game."

He flashed us the big Micky grin. "If they're half as cocky as we've heard, they'll come looking for us. And we can let them walk right into our trap."

"Makes sense," I said. The rules in our paintball wars were simple. Each team had a flag, which it planted somewhere in the tunnels. The team who found and captured the other team's flag without getting shot was the winner. "Are we going to use the central location by the underground phone lines?"

"You got it," Micky said. "Sooner or later they have to pass through that area. Lisa and I mapped out everyone's ambush spot."

Usually, I stayed behind to guard our flag while Lisa and Micky went looking to capture the other team's flag. Lisa didn't like to be alone in the tunnels because she got turned around too easily. With the mousetrap plan, though, we played it different. Even if we had to sit for hours without moving, we would all wait in hiding spots to gun down the other team's soldiers as they moved in on the bait, our flag. Not until most of them were gone would we go hunting for their flag.

"Remember, it's dark," Micky said. "Don't make any guesses. If you see or hear someone coming and you don't hear the password, fire away."

During our paintball wars, we all wore helmets with visors to protect our heads from paint bullets. In the dark tunnels, it was hard to see if a person was an enemy or friend.

"Today's password?" I asked.

"Stinkpot," Micky said.

"Stinkpot?" I repeated.

Micky grinned. "In honor of Joey's fall into the duck pond."

I grinned back. Joey grinned too. I noticed that Lisa didn't.

We walked in silence for the last five minutes. We reached the drainage ditch. There were trees on both sides. It was dry, so we walked along the bottom of the ditch toward the big hill.

As we walked, we had to step over things that had gotten left behind as the runoff water dropped. There were tattered dolls. Plenty of garbage. Old shoes. Plastic pop bottles. All of it had washed from the streets and floated out through the tunnels.

We got to the culvert entrance. There was a cage door of iron bars in front. The bars were welded together in foot-wide squares. Dried grass and weeds had wrapped around the bars on the bottom half of the door. They got stuck on the bars when water flowed through.

The gate was attached to the tunnel with large hinges. It was supposed to be locked, but the lock was old and had been loose for as long as we could remember. To get into the tunnel, all you had to do was jiggle the lock until it popped. Then you just pulled the gate open a bit and slipped inside.

Micky reached for the lock and slapped it a few times until it opened. He tested the gate by pulling it back. It creaked on rusty hinges.

"Where are they?" Lisa demanded. "You don't think they chickened out, do you?"

Before any of us could answer, there was movement in the bushes on the hill above us.

"Chicken? I don't think so," a voice called out.

The Medford school warriors stepped into sight with flashlights attached to their belts, their paintball guns ready, and their helmets in their hands.

Four of them. Big kids. None of them smiled as they looked down on us.

Eight

It didn't bother me that they were big. The tunnels were the only place where I wasn't scared of big kids. Their size worked against them. Skinny, small, and fast—like me—was much better. And like I always said, a good paintball shot knocked the big ones out of the game the same way it did anyone else.

"Hey," Micky said. "Come on down."

The team waited until the guy in front nodded. He had a crew cut and looked like he shaved. He also looked like the kind of guy who had military recruiting posters in his bedroom.

Mr. Military marched his team down. They came down in single file. When Mr. Military stopped, his team stopped. They stood straight and unmoving, with their feet close together and arms at their sides. Paintball guns in one hand. Helmets hanging by the straps from the other hand.

"At ease, men," he said.

All at the same time, they relaxed and moved their feet shoulder-width apart.

At ease? What kind of freaks were these guys?

Micky shot me a look with his eyebrows raised. Then he stepped over and shook Mr. Military's hand.

Micky always surprised me when he did things like that. Around adults, he had an attitude. With anyone our age, though, you'd think he was running for student council.

"You know the rules," Micky said.

"Go over them again so everyone here agrees to them," Mr. Military said. It sounded like he was clipping his words off with scissors.

"Jim," Micky said to me. "The trophy."

I opened my guitar case. Beside my paintball gun was our small flag. It was attached to a short wooden pole. I lifted it out and waved it.

"Our flag," Micky said. "If you take it from us, it's yours. And it will make you kings of the tunnel. No one has managed to capture it from us since the games started last year."

Mr. Military spun and pointed to one of his guys. The guy saluted. I mean, he actually *saluted.* Then he reached inside his jacket and took out their team flag.

"Good," Micky said. "We both put our flags somewhere in sight, somewhere in the tunnels. The war is over when one team takes the other's flag and makes it back here safe. If we take your flag, we add it to our collection. And you can try to get it back next time. But there's a list to take us on again. It might be a couple of months of Saturdays before you get the chance."

"Whatever," Mr. Military said. "I'm not worried. Our guys are tough."

I wondered if they were tunnel tough. It's a different world in there, with the smallest sound echoing from every direction.

"No paint bullets above the shoulders, right?" Mr. Military asked. It was their army against ours. As we tried to take their flag, we would also be trying to put their soldiers out of the game.

"Right," Micky said. "Someone shoots high, they're out, you're still in."

We weren't stupid. Paintball bullets hurt bad enough anywhere else on your body. The last place you want to get hit is in the throat.

"Arms and legs are half hits?" Mr. Military asked.

"Yep," Micky told him. "It takes two shots in the arms or legs to put you out. But a shot to the stomach, chest, or back is an instant kill. Dead soldiers come back out here and wait for the game to end."

"We got it," the Medford guy said. "What else?"

Micky looked at his watch. "You guys are the challengers, so you get first chance to set up. We'll give you thirty minutes to hide your flag before we go into the tunnels. Then you wait where you are and give us thirty minutes. We'll begin looking for each other in exactly one hour. After that, anyone moving in the tunnels is fair game. Good luck."

Mr. Military rubbed his chin. "We don't need luck."

"If you say so," Micky said. He pointed at the sky. "One other thing. It's clear now, but you never know in an hour or two. If it starts to rain and you see *any* water in the tunnels, the game is off. Even if one team is up by three warriors. Everyone leaves the tunnels and we come back to fight another day. Got it?"

"Got it." Mr. Military turned and faced his soldiers.

"Men, prepare for battle," he barked.

All at the same time, they put on their helmets. Like they were robots.

"Full turn," Mr. Military barked.

They all turned toward the black hole of the tunnel. They didn't move toward it yet though.

"Move out, men," Mr. Military commanded.

The Medford guys began to march. The guy who reached the tunnel first held the door open so the others could slip inside. One by one, they marched into the darkness of the tunnel. Because they were so big, they had to crouch once they were inside. I wondered how hard it was to march while crouching.

We heard Mr. Military bark out another order. This time his voice had a weird echo to it from the concrete walls of the tunnel.

"Let the operation begin," he said.

The echo of their footsteps continued to reach us long after they had disappeared into the darkness.

And then there was silence, broken only by the whistling of the wind in the trees.

Nine

Still outside, we waited twenty-five minutes before we opened our guitar cases and took out our paintball guns. There was no sense in having our weapons out in the open, just in case anybody wandered along and decided to ask questions.

We loaded our paintballs. Think of tiny water balloons filled with paint. That's what a paintball bullet is. An expensive paintball gun is accurate up to thirty yards away.

Does it hurt to get hit by a paintball? About like getting hit by a tennis ball—a fast tennis ball.

After we loaded our paintball guns, we took our helmets from our backpacks. We put the helmets on, visors up. We checked our flashlights. Then we were ready. We counted down the final seconds.

Exactly thirty minutes after the Medford team had gone into the tunnels, we followed. Micky held the gate open for the rest of us. He let it fall behind him. We cautiously stepped forward into the darkness.

Twenty steps into the tunnel, we stopped and waited for our eyes to get used to the dark. We had not put the visors down on our helmets yet. There was no need. We had half an hour to get ready for battle.

As we adjusted to the dark, I took a deep breath. Like always, I felt fear, like a ball of wriggling spiders, settle into my stomach. To squash the spiders, I reminded myself of who I was.

Zantor, soldier of the galaxy, has nerves of cold steel bands as he faces a trip deep into the alien nest. The freedom of the citizens of the entire galaxy depends on him. But Zantor will defeat the enemy. Zantor has never failed.

"Jim," Micky whispered. "Take us there, buddy."

"Sure," I said. I promised myself I would get back to Zantor as soon as I had a chance.

I slipped to the front of our short line and started deeper into the darkness. My friends followed. All of us wore Nike's with soft soles. The loudest sound I heard was the sound of my own breath in my helmet.

I was the only one who didn't have to duck as we walked through the cool tunnel. That was one thing that really helped me get around down there.

The other thing was my mind map. I knew exactly where to go.

For some reason, I am good at making maps in my head. All I do is pretend I'm a bird looking down. I keep track of turns and twists in my head, and I never seem to get lost in the tunnels.

Not that getting lost for long is something anyone would have to worry about. For one thing, it's not totally dark. Every forty or fifty steps, there are grates overhead. Or in some tunnels, manhole covers. These openings not only let in water, but they also let in light.

Also, there is a difference in size between the main tunnel and all the others. The main tunnel is big enough to walk through. The tunnels that lead into the main tunnel get slightly smaller. Even smaller tunnels lead into those, and most of those even I have to crawl through.

So if you ever want to get out, you just follow a small tunnel to a bigger tunnel, and a bigger tunnel to the main tunnel. Because some of the bigger tunnels connected with others the same size, it's fairly easy to get confused. But there is a simple test to figure out which way to go.

Drop a marble.

All the tunnels tilt slightly downhill toward the main tunnel. If they didn't, the water would never drain toward the river. Watch which way the marble slowly rolls, and you'll know which way to go.

Of course, we didn't want out. We wanted to reach the central part of the tunnels. Which is why my mind map was so helpful. I knew exactly how to get us there.

I turned my flashlight on and hung it from the back of my pants. I could see enough from the sunlight coming through the grates to know where I was going, so I didn't need the flashlight myself. By hanging it behind me, everyone else could follow me easily.

As we walked beneath each grate, we passed through beams of sunlight. It was colder in the tunnel than in the world above. Mist seemed to hang in those sunlight beams. The soft squeaking of our tennis shoes made a weird sound as it bounced off the concrete walls of the tunnel. And the air smelled like a mixture of dirty socks and rotting tomatoes.

Even with my mind map, I didn't like it much here. Above us were buses and cars. The concrete of the tunnels was old and cracked in places. It had rained a lot over the last month. I wondered if the dirt was heavy with water and ready to collapse the old concrete.

Then my mind really started working. I told myself it could rain hard and fast—we'd be trapped in floodwater. Rats could swarm us. Or maybe there might be snakes. And you always heard about alligators let loose in the sewer tunnels below New York, maybe—

STOP! I told myself.

This was Zantor, galaxy soldier, leading his troops. He feared nothing.

I turned my mind back to where we'd set the mousetrap. It was pretty far ahead in the semidarkness, where three tunnels joined the main tunnel, like spokes at the center of a wheel.

In the center of the joint, the holes in a manhole cover gave good light. That's where we would plant our flag. It would be easy to see. It would draw the Medford guys like mice on cheese.

And we would be hiding in the side tunnels, ready to gun them down.

That, at least, was the plan.

Ten

About ten minutes later, after a lot of twists and turns, we arrived at the place we called the mousetrap. The light coming through the circles in the manhole cover made ghostly white plates on the tunnel floor. The rumble of cars overhead was hardly louder than the sound of someone clearing a throat.

For a few seconds, none of us spoke. Something about being in the tunnels always made us quiet.

"All right," Micky finally whispered. "Jim, buddy, you plant the flag."

There was a ladder coming down from the manhole so workers could get into the tunnel. I climbed halfway up the ladder. With an old shoelace, I tied the flagpole to one of the ladder rungs. A shaft of light fell on the edge of the flag.

I climbed back down.

"Good," Micky said. "Now we guard it. Lisa, you give everyone the directions we went through last night."

"You all packed blankets, right?" she asked.

"Yep," Micky said. "Lying on the cold concrete would be horrible without one."

"Exactly," she said. There were small sections of the maze that Lisa knew like the back of her hand. She just needed help getting to them. Lisa pointed down at a smaller tunnel. "You take that one. Follow it until you come to the cross tunnel. When you get there, lie on the ground. And remember, no noise."

Micky left, ducking to move through the smaller opening. I was always amazed when he took orders from Lisa. But then again, it wasn't fun to disagree with her either.

"Joey . . ." She sounded scornful. "You take the far tunnel on the left. If you go about fifteen steps up it, you'll find a big breaker box. You can hide behind that."

Not only were these tunnels used to drain water, but they also held a lot of underground pipes and wiring, high above the water level.

"Sure," Joey answered in a cheerful voice. It sounded like he was going to do his best to remain sweet, no matter how Lisa treated him. But his voice faltered a bit when he said, "A breaker box?"

"For telephone wires," I told him. "There's no danger from electricity."

"Cool," Joey said.

Lisa ordered him around like he was a five-year-old. "Take your spot. Wait there and don't move until one of us calls you out. Don't even scratch your nose. Your best chance is if they don't know you're there."

"Gotcha," Joey said, cheerful again. "Whatever it takes."

He disappeared into the darkness.

"I'll cover the third small tunnel," Lisa told me. "You keep an eye on the main tunnel behind us. They'll probably try to circle around and come in from one of the smaller tunnels. But they might try the direct approach from the main one to catch us off guard."

"I take my usual spot?" I asked.

"Yep," she said. "You're our ace in the hole. If they get past any of us, we need you to be good. Real good."

No fears, I thought. *Zantor is the best.*

In a few seconds, Lisa was just a dark shadow. Then nothing.

I went to the side of the main tunnel. Large plastic pipes ran along the wall. I guessed these held television cables, protecting them from any water damage.

More important, they were great protection for me. I could slide underneath them and be totally out of sight.

If any of the Medford warriors managed to get this far, I would wait until they were halfway up the ladder. Then I would roll from under the pipes and come out firing paintball bullets.

I set my paintball rifle down and pulled a blanket out of my backpack. It would make my wait on the concrete easier. I knelt down and smoothed the blanket on the rough floor of the tunnel. Then I crawled onto it. I hoped no bugs waited to drop into my ear from the pipes above.

I checked my Indiglo Timex. Eight minutes until the battle began.

I thought of the Medford warriors. Somewhere in the maze of tunnels they were about to start hunting us down. Would they spread out? Or would they come at us in a wave?

The spiders of fear began to wriggle again in my stomach.

Zantor lives for moments like this. Moments that would strain a lesser man's heart to the point of failure. Zantor has no fear. None. The most awesome warrior in the galaxy feeds upon the fear of others.

The spiders of fear went away.

I was glad for the sunlight that squeezed through the small holes in the manhole cover. Without those pale circles of light, the tunnel would have been completely dark.

Zantor strains his razor-sharp hearing for the approach of aliens. Zantor waits with patience. Zantor is the greatest hunter of them all.

I waited. And I waited some more. I checked my Timex again. Still four minutes to war.

When I did hear the sounds, it took me a moment to understand what they were in the echoes of the tunnel.

Blam! Blam! Blam!

It was the thud of paintball bullets.

Followed by a loud scream of pain.

As the scream died, I heard the pounding of feet running down the tunnel. Away from me.

Eleven

At first, I did nothing. Not because I was afraid. I was too busy trying to figure things out to be afraid.

Beyond me, in the darkness, I heard moaning.

"Oh man," a voice croaked. "It hurts. I can hardly breathe. Help me. Help."

Still I did nothing. Maybe the Medford warriors were trying to fake us out. A month earlier, against another team, we had done the same thing—pretended to be hurt. When the team came out of hiding, we splattered them with paintballs.

"Micky?" the voice croaked. "Lisa? Jimmy? Help me . . ."

Using names didn't mean anything. The Medford guys knew all of us by name. Anyone who played paintball did. The Sewer Rats were legends among the warriors. It would be easy for one of them to call out our names to try to fool us.

"Come on. I can't see. Jimmy, help me. Please . . . Lisa? . . . Micky? . . ."

The voice died again, like whoever was calling could hardly get enough air into his lungs.

Zantor, soldier of the galaxy, was hidden in the battlefield, ready to ambush. He heard his name. Was it an alien trick? Or did someone truly need Zantor? Zantor must think quickly.

All right. If it was Micky, he wouldn't have called out his own name. Same with Lisa. So if it was one of us, it had to be Joey.

"Blind . . . help . . . hurry . . ."

Sounds can fool you in the tunnels. They bounce off the walls, and you never know where they're coming from. It could be Joey at the breaker box. Or it could be one of the Medford warriors, somewhere else.

Were the aliens trying to lure Zantor into the open?

"Please . . . please . . ."

If he was acting, this guy was doing a great job.

What would Zantor do?

I decided to take the risk. If it was a trick, the Medford warriors wouldn't find me just by following my voice. I was too well hidden beneath the pipes. And the tricky sound echoes would also fool them.

"Joey?" I called out. "Is that you?"

"Hurry man! . . . It hurts!"

"What's the password?" I asked, raising my voice.

"Stink . . . pot . . ."

This was no trick!

I rolled out from under the pipe. I got to my feet and snapped on my flashlight as I began to run toward Joey's hiding spot.

Within seconds, I reached him. He had fallen beside the breaker box. Clumps of dirt were scattered on the ground beside him. There was also dirt on his shoulders. Even though it was strange to see the dirt, that wasn't what got my attention.

My flashlight beam showed fresh red paint splattered all over the wall behind him.

I lowered the light to Joey's face. And I saw exactly why he was in so much pain.

He'd taken the paintball bullets in the head. That shouldn't have hurt him—except the visor of his helmet had been open.

Red paint covered his face like blood. I was worried some of it might not be paint.

"Hang in there," I told him. "We'll get you out right away."

He nodded and gulped. Then his eyes closed.

"Micky!" I shouted down the tunnels. "Micky! We need help!"

Twelve

Of all the luck, on Monday our baseball schedule had us up against those same jerks from Medford. I shivered as I stood in the dugout and watched them take the field for the first inning. It was a cold day. The sky was dull with dark clouds, and a sharp wind tossed bits of paper across the field.

I watched most closely the four military wanna-bes from the paintball war. They fanned out, three taking the bases and the fourth heading for shortstop. They wore big, cocky smiles, like they had this game wrapped up even before it had started.

I really, really wanted to win this game. I cared. I wanted to knock the ball down their throats and trample them into the dirt. Joey was in the hospital. The four goons had actually laughed about it to me and Lisa and Micky during the warm-up.

Micky must have felt the anger I did.

He's a great athlete—when he cares to try. Not only

that, but he's also a great team leader. You can't help but look up to him. He's big and strong and doesn't act like he's cool because of it.

Micky was first up to bat. He stopped in front of our team before walking out to the plate. "You all heard what some of these guys did to Joey. Let's give them their first loss of the season," Micky said quietly.

I couldn't help noticing Coach Martin's small, satisfied smile as the rest of us cheered.

Micky led off with a double deep into right field. He almost went for a triple but decided to hold up at second. Lisa bunted a sacrifice, moving him to third. Their pitcher walked me, and just like that, we had two runners on with only one out.

Our fourth batter went down swinging, but when Rainbow got to the plate, he made up for it with a homer that put us up 3–0. The score stayed that way for five more innings. All the hours of practice paid off as our fielding began to click behind Micky's strong pitching.

The real first scoring chance for the Medford jerks came in the bottom of the sixth. They had one man down and runners on first and second. We were playing in our new positions—Micky pitching, me at shortstop. One of the military boys slapped a fastball that bounced to my left. I snagged it with a backhand, then flipped it to Lisa at second. She tagged the bag and set herself to throw to first for the double play.

The runner coming in hard from first was one of the other military jerks. I saw his face clearly as he did a hook slide into second. He was grinning, looking to spike Lisa's legs and take her out before she could complete the double play.

She saw it coming too. She jumped to miss his spikes and held on to the ball to keep from throwing wild. She landed with both shoes on his hand, giving his fingers a double set of spikes as payback. As he howled in pain, she spun and fired the ball at home plate. Although their hitter had made it safely to first, their base runner from second had rounded third and decided to go for home. He was two steps short of the plate when the throw beat him and the catcher tagged him out.

End of inning.

As Lisa helped the military jerk to his feet, she smiled sweetly. "I am so sorry," she said. "It was a total accident. After all, you know us girls. We can't do anything right in baseball."

Their pitcher was good. He threw screwballs and floaters that dipped like butterflies around the plate. Our first-inning hits must have stung him into really concentrating, because he put us down 1-2-3 in nearly every inning that followed, including the seventh and eighth. Meanwhile, they scored two runs in the eighth by taking advantage of an outfield error after three straight singles before Micky found his fastball again.

We started batting in the ninth ahead 3–2. It was

fun to be playing solid baseball. I was the leadoff hitter. I wanted a hit so badly that I didn't wait on the first two pitches and swung wildly at them both. The pitcher must have figured I would be just as big a sucker on the next pitches. He kept his next three pitches way outside, but I just watched them go by for balls.

That's where the count stood. Three balls. Two strikes. I stood and waited for the payoff pitch. Maybe he was thinking an inside fastball would catch me sleeping after I'd watched three go by. But he lost control and the pitch came in too sharp. In a split second, I knew it would hit me. I also knew I had just enough time to throw myself back. Instead, I gritted my teeth and turned into the ball, taking it on the meat of my shoulder.

"Take your base," the umpire called.

As I trotted to first base, I wondered if I had gone crazy. I'd actually let a pitch hit me.

I repeated it to myself.

I'd actually let a pitch hit me.

This was the result of caring so much?

On first base, the wind was still sharp on my face. While the crowd cheered for their pitcher to strike out our next batter, I wanted to rub my shoulder.

It hurt. Bad.

But with the military goon standing beside me, I wasn't going to show any pain.

"Loser," he said. "Leave baseball to us. We'll leave car theft to you guys."

As a point of record, I have never stolen a car. Neither has Micky. Or Lisa. Or any of my teammates. "If we stole cars like you jerks played baseball," I said, "we'd run out of gas at the first stop sign."

"Very funny," he said. "As funny as that friend of yours ending up in the hospital."

He spit. "Losers."

He was twice my size. But I came real close to trying to tackle him. Only years of fear managed to keep my anger from winning.

I said nothing else. As the pitcher got set for his throw, I took a good lead off first base. He spun and the ball screamed toward first. I dived back, just barely avoiding the pick-off attempt.

"Loser," the military goon said again as I stood up.

My anger came real close to taking over.

Zantor wants to destroy the alien creature with his bare hands.

As I leaned over to dust off my pants, he threw the ball back to the pitcher. I heard the thwack as the ball hit the pitcher's glove.

Zantor will find another way to destroy the alien.

Like stealing second. That would show this guy who the real loser was.

I took another big lead off first.

"Hey shorty," he said, standing on the bag.

I glared at him. "What?"

"There's this old trick in baseball," he said. "While the runner isn't looking, the first baseman pretends to throw the ball back to the pitcher. The pitcher pops his glove with his bare hand to make the sound of catching a ball. But really, the first baseman has the ball the whole time."

He grinned a big, cocky grin and showed me the ball in his hand. Before I could move, he stepped forward and tagged me.

"You're out," he said. "Loser."

The rest of his team split their sides laughing.

Our next two batters struck out, sitting us down again, 1-2-3.

The Medford team scored twice in the bottom of the ninth, a single followed by a homer, putting them up 4–3. And that was the end of the game.

The Medford players swarmed the pitcher like they had just won the World Series.

I felt bitter juice in the pit of my stomach. I'd wanted to win so badly that for a moment, in the pain of defeat, I wanted to run my head into a wall. By the way Micky and Lisa walked with their shoulders slumped, I saw they were just as disappointed.

As we walked off the field, I realized why I always made sure not to care too much. The thing about hoping for something, I decided in that cold wind beneath gray skies, is that all you do is set yourself up for disappointment.

Thirteen

I hate hospitals. I think it's from all the times my parents dragged me around with them when they made calls on sick people. We should try to help those in need, they always say. Fine, but it would be nice if I could decide for myself once in a while. From the time I was little, I remember the smells and the big hallways and people in white walking fast in all directions. Most of all—especially when I was little—I remember how afraid hospitals made me feel because everyone around me seemed so afraid.

On Tuesday afternoon, all of those feelings came back to me as Micky and I looked for Joey's room in the hospital. Plus, I was already nervous because of what had happened to Joey. I wanted to throw up.

Zantor does his duty in remaining by the side of a fallen comrade.

Micky must have been nervous too. He didn't say much either. Not until we got to room 1875.

"We should have brought him comic books or something," Micky said.

"Except what if he can't read?" I asked. That was my big fear—that Joey was blind. He'd taken paint-ball bullets in the face. Not good.

On Saturday, while Micky had helped Joey out of the tunnel, I had run ahead to find a pay phone to call for an ambulance. Then I called his folks, who went straight to the hospital to meet him. Our last view of Joey had been as the paramedics loaded him into the ambulance. This afternoon, we had no idea what to expect.

Micky knocked on the door.

"Come in," a man's voice said.

We pushed through the door.

Joey lay in bed, wearing his pajamas. He had a white eye patch taped over his left eye. The other side of his face was the color of mushed prunes.

I gulped.

A man who had been sitting beside Joey's bed stood up. He was big, with dark hair, a wide face, and a thick mustache. He had a mole on his left cheek. He wore blue jeans and a sweatshirt.

"I'm Joey's father," he said. "John Saylor."

For some reason, I felt like I had seen him before.

"Micky Downs," Micky said to him. Micky didn't go over and shake the man's hand. Micky doesn't like anyone who has authority. That includes all adults.

"Jim McClosky," I said, standing a little behind Micky.

62

No recognition showed on the man's face, so I decided I was wrong about seeing him before.

"Hey guys," Joey said. His voice sounded much better. "Dad, these two helped me get out of the tunnel."

I winced. Enough trouble had already come down on us from the adults in our lives. It looked like we'd never have another paintball game again. Now I figured it was Joey's father's turn to lecture us.

But instead of frowning and ripping into us, Joey's father smiled.

"I want to thank you guys for your quick thinking in there. You made all the right moves."

I found my voice. "You're not mad at us?"

"A little," the man said, "but from what Joey explained, you guys made sure everyone playing the paintball games followed safety rules. It was just a bad break that Joey hadn't closed his visor."

"A real bad break," Joey said. "I think my watch was a little slow. I thought I still had a few minutes, so I had my visor half open to breathe better. I was sitting against the wall, and boom, out of nowhere two guys appeared and started firing. It was like they knew exactly where I was."

He touched his face. "Good thing the bullets caught the edge of my visor. It slowed some of the impact. Otherwise I might have lost an eye."

I pointed at his eye patch. "You can see?"

"The doctor says everything will be fine in a few days," Joey told me.

"Again, thanks to you guys getting him out so fast," his dad said. He smiled at Micky. "Of course, that shouldn't be a surprise. I've heard of your father. He was quite a hero."

Micky looked back at him. An angry expression crossed Micky's face. He opened his mouth to say something. Then he changed his mind and closed his mouth. He turned around and left the room without saying a word.

"Did I say something wrong?" Mr. Saylor asked.

"Yeah," I said, "but it's not your fault."

Once, and only once, Micky had spoken to me about his dad, the policeman. At an accident, he'd gone into a burning car to rescue a woman. And the car had exploded. Micky thought heroes were useless. He said he'd rather have a live father than someone everyone else called a hero.

Micky was mad at his dad for dying. And he got mad at anyone who said he should be proud that his dad had given up his life while trying to help someone else.

"What did I say?" Mr. Saylor asked. "What made him mad?"

"It's not a big deal," I said.

It was, of course. But it was Micky's business who he told about his father, not mine.

"Well," I said, "I've got to go. Get better, Joey."

That was the end of the hospital visit.

I found Micky in the hallway. He was pacing from one side to another.

I didn't say anything. Micky burns slow. I didn't figure talking would do any good.

"I've been thinking," Micky said when he looked up at me. "We've got to go."

"Sure," I said. If he wanted to pretend nothing had happened in the hospital room, that was fine. "Where?"

"Let me ask you something. Did you hear what Joey told us? About when he got hit?"

"I was right there with you," I said. "I'm not deaf."

"Well?" Micky asked.

"Well what?" I asked back.

"Joey said it was like the guys knew exactly where he was."

"And?" I said.

"If Joey's watch was a little slow, they probably fired as soon as they knew it was time to start the paintball war. You know, right on the hour. Like they *did* know exactly where he was. Like they were waiting to gun him down as soon as they could."

It hit me. If that was true, there was only one way they could have known where he would be.

"You don't think . . ."

"Yes, I do." He smiled grimly. "Which is why we are leaving this hospital right now."

 *Fourteen*

But we didn't leave the hospital. At least, not right away.

We were halfway down the hall to the elevator when the doors opened and Coach Martin stepped out.

Without his sweats, he almost didn't look like Coach. He wore blue jeans and a white T-shirt, looking like a normal guy, not some social worker or preacher type. He carried a couple of books.

"Hey guys," he said. "How's Joey?"

"Okay, I guess," I said. I frowned. "How did you know he was here?"

He smiled. "Lisa told me."

Lisa? I didn't get it. Lisa didn't trust anyone. And even if she trusted Coach Martin enough to talk to him, why would she talk about Joey? She *hated* Joey.

"Anyway," he said, lifting his hand with the books, "I thought I'd bring him these. I know what it's like to spend time in a hospital with nothing to do."

"Books?" Micky said with suspicion. "What are you trying to teach him?"

"Nothing," Coach Martin said, half laughing. "These are sports books. Unless it's something you need to study for school, why read unless you enjoy it?"

"What a concept," Micky said. "Reading for fun. What next, needles in the eyeballs—for fun?"

I expected Coach Martin to get mad. Instead, he laughed louder. "You poor guy. I can't imagine what's been forced on you over the years. *Little Women? Anne of Green Gables?* Great books, but they're a little light on action."

Micky actually smiled.

We started to walk away.

"Hang on a sec," I said to Micky. I turned around. "Coach Martin?"

He was nearly at Joey's room. "Yes?"

I walked back toward him. "How do you know what it's like to spend time in a hospital?"

"Long story. It's about a stupid kid and a motorcycle."

"Try me," I said.

Micky had drifted in closer. He hates to show interest in anything, but the fact that he had almost joined us told me he wanted to hear too.

"The stupid kid was me," Coach Martin said. "I was nineteen and ready to take on the world."

"You were a major-league prospect?" I asked.

Coach Martin raised his eyebrows.

"That's what that officer said," I added.

The coach nodded. "Something like that," he answered. "I'm sure I wasn't as good as I thought I was, but there were teams interested in signing me."

"And then?" This from Micky. I was surprised. Micky tried to never seem interested when adults talked.

"I drank too much beer one night, drove too fast, and hit a tree. Broke my leg in three places. Ended my baseball career before it got started. But I was lucky. At least I lived."

"You? Beer?" I couldn't believe my ears.

Again, that wonderful laugh of his. He pulled his sleeve up and turned his arm.

A tattoo. Wow.

"Gang markings," he said. "From when I lived on the streets, growing up in east L.A. I did plenty then that I'm not proud of now."

"But . . . but . . ." Micky was sputtering.

"Bible thumper?" he asked. "Goody two-shoes?"

Micky blushed slightly. "Yeah," he said. "If you were that cool then . . ."

"That's the deal," Coach Martin said. "It wasn't cool. Hurting people? Lying? Stealing? That motorcycle accident almost killed me. It made me ask a lot of questions. Like why I felt so empty and angry and scared if my life was so cool."

He shrugged. "What I found was a man who died on a cross, who gave His life for me. I found the God who created this universe and discovered how lonely my soul was without Him."

"Bible thumper," Micky snarled. "I was wondering when you'd get around to this."

Bible thumper. That's what I had been afraid of all season—being called a Bible thumper. That's why I had kept real quiet about any of this, even though my parents kept telling me I was supposed to be trying to help Micky and Lisa. But Bible thumpers weren't cool.

"Hang on," Coach Martin said. "You were the one asking questions. And if you listen close, you'll hear I'm not telling you what to do. I'm just telling you what I found."

"He's got a point, Micky," I said. After all, more than half of the season had passed, and Coach Martin had done nothing more than be there for us. He hadn't tried to preach at all.

"This church stuff," Micky said, "I don't buy it. I could tell you so many stories about church people who were bigger jerks than anyone else I've met."

"Big difference between a church and personal faith," Coach Martin said. "One's a building filled with people who sometimes get so caught up in rules they forget what's important. The other is about trying to understand life and why God put you here . . . about believing that you have a soul ready to be filled with love, and that there's only one place and one way to find that love."

"Come on," Micky said to me. "He's preaching."

"He's not," I said. I tried to make a joke. "When he starts calling you a sinner, that's when he's preaching."

Again, unexpectedly, Coach Martin laughed. "You two are bright kids. You've got good hearts. I was glad to see you decide to play baseball instead of just go through the motions. You can both go a long way if you set your mind on it."

I felt bad that I'd done such a good job of pretending not to care that Coach Martin thought I was like the rest of the Tigers.

Coach Martin drew a breath. "Tell you what. Any time you have questions, you just ask. I'm not saying I have the answers, but I'll do my best."

What a cool thing to say. He wasn't forcing anything on Micky. But he was giving him a chance to ask questions.

Micky put both his hands on his hips and stared at Coach Martin.

"All right," Micky said. "How's this for a question? Why'd my dad decide it was more important to be a dead hero than to be with the family who needed him? His dying for someone else was stupid."

For a couple of seconds, Coach Martin couldn't think of a thing to say.

Micky grabbed my arm. "Come on," he said to me. "Let's go."

Coach Martin didn't try to stop us.

Fifteen

I met Micky that night just outside the 7-Eleven.

"Hey," he said.

"Hey," I answered. From the hospital we'd gone straight to Lisa's house. But she hadn't been there. And she wasn't here now. "Where's Lisa?"

"Couldn't get hold of her," he said. "Her mom said she was in her room and didn't want to talk to anyone."

I nodded. I understood. When Lisa got into one of her bad moods, she was like a bear with a toothache. I wondered if this bad mood had anything to do with Joey. And if it had anything to do with what we thought she might have done to him.

"Well," he said.

"Well," I said. I had something I wanted to bring up with Micky. I just wasn't sure when or how to begin.

We sat on the curb for a while, watching people drive up, get out of their cars, look down their noses at us on the way into the 7-Eleven, look down their noses at us on the way out of the 7-Eleven, get back in their cars, and drive away.

"This isn't much fun," I finally said.

"What isn't?"

"Hanging out here. I mean, it's starting to seem useless."

"Then what do you suggest?" By his voice, it seemed Micky was in a bad mood too.

"Let's talk about the television set and the stereo," I said. "Maybe you shouldn't have done it. Maybe you can take them back."

There. I had said it. Maybe it wasn't the best way to bring it up, but at least I had said it.

"Take back the television set and stereo," Micky said slowly. He stared at me. "Have you lost your mind?"

"I dunno," I said. What I really wanted to say was that Micky had become my best friend. Maybe he was a Tiger and everyone else thought he was a loser. But I liked him a lot. I wished he wasn't so mad about life.

"It's that Bible-thumping Coach Martin, isn't it?" he sneered. "He's turning you into a wimp too. I thought you were different from those church people."

Zantor faces the judges of a world delegation. Zantor must argue his case or get thrown into a cage of intergalactic electric eels.

"That's just it," I said. "He's *not* a Bible thumper. He's just a good guy. All season the Tigers have treated him like dirt, and all he's done is tried to help. He never once got mad. Never once lectured. Never once

74

started quoting Bible stuff like he was better than us. And if he was once in a street gang but now . . ."

I didn't finish my sentence. But I had been thinking a lot since we'd left the hospital. Angry inside? Scared? Empty? If I were honest, that described me and Micky. Micky's angry. I'm scared. Coach Martin, though, had this peace that nothing seemed to shake. Like church wasn't just some kind of club. Like what he believed was worth something. Like maybe I should look at my parents in a new light.

Micky stood up. He spit on the ground.

"Man," he said, "I can't believe you fell for his line. Judges, police, teachers, and preachers, they're all the same. They keep telling us what to do—with no idea what it's really like for us."

He spit again. "I don't need you. I don't need Lisa. I don't need anyone."

I watched him walk away. I watched his shadow as he passed under a streetlight. I watched him turn a corner and disappear.

I sure felt alone.

Sixteen

Yesterday's wind had become colder. Low dark clouds hung heavy in the sky. There was nothing to enjoy about my bike ride with Micky from school to Lisa's house. Not the weather. Not Micky's continued silence since our fight the night before. Especially not what Micky and I knew we had to ask Lisa.

Lisa's mother answered the door of their small house.

"Hello boys," she said. Mrs. Chambers pushed her hair out of her face. She was blond like Lisa, but her face was tired. "You two aren't here to take Lisa to another paintball war or anything, are you?"

"No ma'am," I said. "We're here to pick her up for a baseball game."

"Baseball is definitely better than paintball," Mrs. Chambers said. "Lisa's in her bedroom, I think. I'll go get her. If you two meet us in the kitchen, I'll fix you all a quick snack before you go."

She gave us a smile. A tired one. But it was still a smile. "Don't think I'm real upset with you about the paintball games. I understand about kids trying to have fun. But I am glad you promised to stay out of that maze of tunnels from now on."

We nodded as we stepped past her into the house.

"How's that boy who got hurt?" she asked.

"He's all right," Micky said. "Joey has to wear an eye patch, but the doctors say he can take it off soon. And his vision should be okay."

She frowned. "Joey? Lisa told me his name was Chuck."

We shrugged. Lisa often said and did things we couldn't figure out.

Micky and I walked into the kitchen as Mrs. Chambers went to get her daughter. We sat at the table to wait.

A half second later, I stood up.

"What?" Micky said.

I pointed at the fridge. There was a framed photo on top.

"Tell your stomach to wait until Lisa and her mom get here," Micky said.

"No. Not the fridge. The photo on top. Look who's in it."

He pushed his chair back and came closer. Then he whistled. "I don't get it. That's Joey's dad."

Micky and I had been in this kitchen before. But I'd never paid close attention to the photograph.

It explained why, in the hospital, I'd thought I'd

seen Mr. Saylor before. It was this photo. Joey's dad was standing on a dock at a lake, holding a big fish in one hand and a fishing rod in the other. Mustache. Mole on his cheek. Beside him, Mrs. Chambers and Lisa both squinted into the sun. It was an old picture, taken when Lisa was much smaller.

"Joey's dad," Micky repeated. "John Saylor. I don't get it."

Before I could say anything, Mrs. Chambers came into the kitchen.

"Lisa's gone," Mrs. Chambers said. She held a piece of paper. She waved it as she spoke. "She left a note saying she'd meet you two at the diamond."

What was with Lisa? She always waited for us. We were the Sewer Rats. All for one and one for all and all that other Three Musketeers stuff.

"We'll look for her there," I said.

"Want a sandwich to go?" Mrs. Chambers asked.

"No thanks," I answered. Micky just shook his head.

I pointed at the fridge and asked, "By the way, who's the man in that picture?"

"Oh," Mrs. Chambers said. "That's Lisa's father."

She stopped for a second. When she spoke again, her voice was quiet. "We haven't been married for a long time. After we got divorced, he left town, and I took my maiden name again. We both started over. He and his new family just moved back to the area."

"Lisa's father," Micky said, too surprised to remember he didn't like to talk to adults. "But the kid in the—"

I elbowed Micky.

"Let's go before it rains," I said to Micky.

"Sure, but—"

I grabbed his arm and pulled before he could tell Mrs. Chambers anything about Joey and the man in the hospital.

This was something Lisa should explain. But if I had guessed right, there wasn't much left to explain.

Seventeen

On the way to the ball field, Micky still didn't say anything about our fight the night before. He rode his bike ahead of me, making sure we didn't have a chance to talk.

I hoped he still wanted to be my friend. But I just didn't know how to get back to where we'd been before he walked away from me.

I didn't ask him about it though. I had plenty on my mind.

Like Lisa.

She would have a lot of explaining to do as soon as the game was over.

It wasn't much of a game. Micky went back to shortstop and let Rainbow pitch again. Coach Martin, as usual, didn't get in our way and tell us how to run the team. He just stood beside the bench and yelled encouragement at us, even though it was obvious we were back to not caring again.

His yelling didn't help. Rainbow gave up fifteen runs on more hits than I could count. We only managed one run, and that was a gift because the left outfielder missed an easy fly ball. We scored on his error.

Although the game only took an hour and a half to play, it seemed to me like five hours.

As we came off the field after the final out, Micky and I caught up to Lisa.

"We want to talk to you," Micky said.

Lisa lifted her chin and stared at us. "About what?" she asked. I could almost see her guard go up.

"About what?" Micky said. "About what Jim and I saw at your house when we came over to pick you up, like we always do. You know, the house you left before your buddies even got there?"

"It's about a photo," I said quietly. "Of you and Joey's father. I think you owe us an explanation."

She glared at us. "I don't owe you a thing."

Micky grabbed her arm. She pulled away.

Before either of us could say anything else, Coach Martin walked up to us.

"Hey Micky," he said. He turned to nod at me. "Jim."

His voice sounded friendly. Either he hadn't seen our argument with Lisa, or he was smart enough to know it was our business.

"Yeah," Micky said.

"I got a call from the police this morning," Coach Martin said.

Lisa walked away. We couldn't follow her—not with Coach Martin talking to us.

"So?" Micky said.

"Seems the house that was broken into last week had another break-in last night."

"What's that to us?" Micky asked, acting his usual cool self.

"Probably nothing," Coach Martin answered, unbothered by Micky's tone. "Just wanted you to know that the police won't be hassling the team about this break-in."

Coach Martin paused. "Seems all the stuff that was stolen got returned."

There was a twinkle in his eye. Like he knew we had something to do with it but wasn't going to say so.

"Probably elves or something," Micky said.

Although I felt like giving Micky a high-five for doing the right thing, I hid my emotion.

We still had Lisa to worry about.

I watched her get on her bike. She rode away without looking back.

"Um, Coach?" I said. "We've got to go."

"Sure," he said. "Don't forget tomorrow's practice."

But we weren't listening. We were already running for our bikes to chase Lisa.

Eighteen

We didn't find Lisa in Bell Park. Instead, we found her bicycle. At the edge of the drainage ditch. Near the sewer tunnel entrance.

"Suppose she went inside?" I asked.

Micky looked at the dark sky. He held his hand out, feeling for drops of rain.

"I hope not," he said. "It could start to rain any second. And rain hard. You know what that means."

I nodded. It meant a lot of water. The drainage ditch was empty now, but during a hard rainstorm, it would be filled with fast, muddy water—higher than my waist. Like a flash flood.

I walked over to the iron gate of the tunnel and looked inside. It was just a black hole. A huge black hole. If she had decided to go into the tunnels, it could be years before we found her. And that was only if she didn't hide.

I thought about the rain. If she was in there, Micky and I needed to warn her. Even if it was dangerous for us.

But if she wasn't in there, we could be putting ourselves in danger for nothing.

"Lisa?" I yelled. "Lisa?"

"Don't yell," said a grumpy voice. "It hurts my ears."

I nearly had a heart attack. I never expected her to be so close. But as my eyes got used to the darkness, I saw her outline. She was sitting just inside the tunnel, about twenty steps away.

"Come on out," Micky said, moving beside me. "We need to talk."

"No," she said.

"No?" Micky asked. "What do you mean, no?"

"It's a two-letter word for buzz off."

From where she was sitting, Micky and I would look like two dark figures against the light of the sky.

"We need to talk," Micky said again.

"Buzz off," she said.

"But—"

"Buzz off," she repeated. "Or don't you understand English? Maybe I should tell you in French."

I smiled a little. Her bicycle spoke more French than she did.

"I came here to be alone," she continued. "I wanted a place where nobody would bug me. So in case you haven't figured it out, *I don't want to talk.*"

"You have to talk," Micky said.

"Why?" came her voice.

"Because we know about you and Joey."

Silence from inside the tunnel.

"We saw his dad in the hospital," Micky told her. "He's the same guy who's in the photograph on your refrigerator."

Silence.

"Not only that," Micky said. "We know it probably wasn't an accident that Joey got hit with those paint-balls."

For a second, there was more silence. But only for a second. Then I heard the pounding of feet as Lisa ran deeper into the tunnel.

"Lisa!" Micky shouted. "Lisa! Stop!"

She didn't. Her echoing footsteps faded. Then there was nothing but the blackness of the tunnel.

"Nuts," Micky said. He kicked at a rock. "Dumb girl."

Before I could say anything, a crack of lightning caught the corner of my eye. Then a crash of thunder rolled over us.

And it began to pour.

Nineteen

Now what!" I yelled above the sound of the rain. Heavy, hard drops pounded my skull. Within seconds, my hair was soaked. I looked like I had stepped into a shower.

Micky didn't answer. He grabbed my arm and pulled me toward the tunnel. He yanked the gate open and pulled me inside, out of the rain.

"At least in here we'll be dry," he said.

Not for long, I thought.

I looked outside. The sky had disappeared. All I saw were gray sheets of water. Already, there were puddles in the drainage ditch. Soon the puddles would join and begin to flow. And water would stream over our feet from the tunnels.

"We've got to get her out of here," I said. "If it doesn't stop raining . . ."

"She's got a brain and two feet," he said. "She can get herself out."

"Come on, Micky. You know she's the one who gets lost the easiest. Remember the day we had to go looking?"

I was telling the truth. And we both knew it. While Lisa knew some parts of the tunnels, her sense of direction was terrible. After one paintball war, it had taken her two hours to find her way out. Since then, she'd stayed with one of us when we'd gone after the other team's flag in battle.

"Look," Micky snapped. "I'm no hero."

"Oh." I knew better than to say anything else.

We waited five minutes in silence.

At least silence from any more talk. All the noise came from the rain. It sounded like an army of drummers.

A small stream of water began to trickle at our feet. Not just from our wet hair and wet clothes. But also from the streets and gutters that fed the tunnels.

I started walking up the tunnel.

"What are you doing?" he asked.

I turned.

"Micky, I'm no hero either. But Lisa knows as much as we do how important it is to clear out when the water starts to run. If she hasn't come back by now, it's because she can't."

"How are you going to find her?" he asked. "There are dozens of smaller tunnels she could have taken."

"I don't know," I said. "But I've got to try."

I knew if something happened to her and I hadn't done my best to help, I would feel guilty for the rest of my life.

"Even if it kills you?" Micky said. His voice sounded angry. "Heroes are stupid. Dead heroes are even stupider."

"Getting killed is not part of my plan," I said. I tried to say it calmly, but as my voice echoed back to me off the walls, it didn't sound calm.

I walked deeper into the tunnel. The stream of water had gotten deeper. Already, it had started to push over the toes of my shoes.

I repeated my words to myself.

Getting killed is not part of my plan.

Twenty

I should have known I'd get scared. I'd been so worried about Lisa and the water, I had forgotten what happens as the darkness closes around me.

After a few more steps into the tunnel, I felt the familiar wriggling of spiders in my stomach. I remembered how I felt when I was a little kid and I woke up in the dark, alone in bed.

Now, just like then, I felt so lonely that my chest hurt.

Except for one difference. Here the noise of the water in the tunnel surrounded me. Water that was growing faster and stronger as all the street gutters above dumped into these tunnels.

As the spiders of fear wriggled, I turned myself into . . .

Zantor!

The soldier of the galaxy will never die. He bats away danger as if it were just a pesky fly. His legs are so strong, no river can sweep him away.

"Jim!" Micky shouted from behind me. "Hang on!"

Zantor paused, glad for help in his noble quest.

"Micky," I said as he caught up to me. "Thanks, man."

"Don't thank me for being stupid. Maybe it's my fault she ran away. You know, because I talked about Joey and her dad."

"It's not your fault," I said. "She can't run away from that stuff forever."

Micky put his hand on my shoulder and squeezed. It made me feel a lot taller.

"So," he said. "Where did she go?"

"My guess is she stayed in the main tunnel as far as possible. If she was trying to get away from us, it's easier to run in this tunnel than in the smaller ones. Besides, she's probably afraid of getting lost in the side tunnels."

We passed beneath a street grate emptying a tiny waterfall from the gutter above. We splashed through the gray light from the grate. We could see the water at our feet spreading into a small stream.

"What if she took a side tunnel?"

"She probably wouldn't have gone in too far. She should be able to hear us."

Ahead, the wall of the tunnel was a little darker, showing where a smaller tunnel ran into ours.

I stopped. "Lisa!" I yelled into the side tunnel. "Where are you?"

We waited a couple of seconds. No answer.

We moved on. By now, the stream had risen to our ankles. Water splashed halfway up my shins.

"Lisa!" Micky yelled at the next tunnel. "Lisa!"

That's how it went for the next few minutes. We stopped and yelled into every tunnel that branched from the main tunnel. I was so scared for her that even Zantor, soldier of the galaxy, was getting afraid.

We reached the mousetrap place in the tunnels, where three other tunnels all joined together. Water poured from the holes in the manhole cover above. The place where I had been lying beneath the plastic pipes was completely covered with water. The stream was halfway up to our knees and sucked at our legs with every step we took.

"Think about it," I said. "We waited about five minutes before coming after her. Running at full speed, she would have gotten this far in five minutes, but not much farther."

"And?"

"About here she would have noticed the water. She would have turned around, right?"

"Right," he said. He had to raise his voice. The rushing sounds of the rising water forced us to talk louder to hear. "So why haven't we seen her yet on her way back?"

I grabbed his arm.

"Listen!" I shouted.

I pointed in the direction I thought the noise had come from.

He turned his head that way, leaning to hear better.

For a few seconds, there was nothing. Only the rush of water.

Then . . .

"Help! . . . Help me!"

It was a faint sound. But there was no mistake. Ahead, from the tunnel to our right, came Lisa's voice.

We almost tripped over each other in our hurry to get there.

We left behind the faint light from the manhole cover as we ran into the darkness ahead.

"Help!" We could hear her clearer now. "Jim! Micky! Help me!"

I was in front. So I hit it first—a solid wall where there should have been tunnel.

Micky smacked into me.

"Hey!" he said. "Why'd you stop?"

"No choice," I shouted at him. "Part of the tunnel wall must have fallen."

I tried to picture it as if I had a flashlight. The dirt above was heavy with all the water from all the rain we'd had. The concrete of the tunnels was old. I remembered that I had seen dirt near here when I'd found Joey. The concrete must have been cracking then. Now it had finally fallen.

"A cave-in," I said to Micky.

He pushed past me. He felt around with his hands. A few seconds later, he spoke to me.

"There's an opening at the top."

"And she's on the other side, right?"

He didn't answer me.

"Lisa!" he shouted. "Can you hear me?"

"Yes, yes, yes!"

"Are you all right?" he shouted.

"My foot is trapped," she said.

"We'll run and get help."

"No!" Even in the confusion of the water and the darkness, the fear in her voice reached us.

"No?"

"The water," she cried. "It's already up to my knees!"

That's when I noticed—the floor on our side was dry. There was no stream running over our feet, no stream adding to the big one in the main tunnel.

And there was only one reason.

This fallen cement and dirt had made more than a wall. It had made a dam, holding all the water on the other side. Rising water. Where Lisa was trapped.

Twenty-One

Zantor thought quickly. Seconds later, Zantor knew what to do.

"Micky," I said. "The opening at the top. Can you tell how big it is?"

I waited a few seconds as he felt around in the dark.

"Big enough to get through," he said, quickly guessing why I had asked.

"Then one of us needs to climb over and help Lisa," I said. "And one of us needs to get out of here and tell someone what's going on. The ladder in the main tunnel reaches a manhole cover. It's the fastest way out."

A clump of dirt fell from the tunnel roof and hit my shoulder. Was another big piece going to cave in?

"Good plan," he said. "But who goes for help?"

The spiders of fear woke up in my stomach again. Whoever stayed behind would have to crawl through the small opening. I imagined the tunnel roof falling down on me.

I wanted to run.

"Who goes for help?" Micky asked again. "I mean, it's not fair to the person who has to stay behind."

"We'll do it this way," I said. "I'm going to put my hand behind my back. I'll hold up one finger. Or two. If you call it right, you go for help. Call it wrong, I go."

"But—"

"Can you think of a better way?"

"No," he said.

I put my hand behind my back. I made a fist and held out one finger.

Micky waited.

"Come on," I said. "Guess. We don't have much time."

"Two," Micky said. "Two fingers."

He had guessed wrong. All I had to do was show him my hand with one finger showing. And I could go free.

I brought my hand from behind my back—with two fingers sticking out from my fist, not one.

"Can you see it in this darkness?" I asked.

He reached for my hand and felt both fingers.

"Two," he said.

A trickle of water ran onto the floor of the tunnel. Somewhere, the wall had sprung a leak. Water from the other side was starting to get through.

"You called it right," I told Micky. "You go for help."

"Are you sure?" he asked.

"Very sure," I said. "That's what we agreed."

Micky was too big. I had a better chance of getting through the hole to Lisa. Plus he was strong enough to push away the manhole cover to get to the street above. As much as I wanted to go, it didn't make sense for him to stay behind. I knew I would never like myself if I ran away now.

"Lisa!" I shouted before I could change my mind. "Hang on! I'm coming over the top!"

I put my hand on Micky's shoulder. "Give me a hand. Get me up to the opening. Then go for help as fast as you can."

Micky boosted me high enough for me to get my head and shoulders into the hole. I pulled forward while he pushed my feet.

The darkness seemed to swallow me in the tight space.

Twenty-Two

I began to breathe fast. It seemed like I couldn't get air deep into my lungs. I wanted to scream.

Lisa beat me to the scream.

"Hurry," she cried from the other side. "The water is nearly up to my waist!"

It was like a slap across my face.

I pulled myself forward. My fingers dug into the dirt. My belly scraped over pieces of concrete. Almost in a panic, I wondered if I would get stuck. I needed . . .

Zantor, soldier of the galaxy. Zantor moves ahead. Zantor is fearless. The odds are against him. Yet because Zantor is fearless he will—

Stop, I told myself.

I was crawling over a cave-in. More of the roof could fall on me any second. On the other side, rising water might drown me, and Lisa. It was okay to be afraid.

In fact, only an idiot *wouldn't* be afraid.

I didn't need Zantor. I needed to get to Lisa and help her. And I needed to not be afraid of being afraid. I needed to keep going.

I thought of Coach Martin and his peace. I thought of Mom and Dad and how they helped people because of what they believed. I made my own choice. I closed my eyes and prayed that God would watch over us.

I opened my eyes again. I pulled myself ahead with new strength, keeping my head down, hoping my shoulders wouldn't get stuck.

Then, without warning, my fingers clawed at air.

"Lisa?"

"Here!"

She was so close, I could almost . . .

I did. I reached down and grabbed her hands.

"Lisa!"

I kicked ahead and began to fall. She kept hold of my hands as I splashed into the water beside her.

It was totally dark.

"Jimmy!" She pulled me close and hugged me. "Jimmy!"

"Micky's gone for help," I said. "I'm going to stay with you."

"He's got to hurry," she said. "The water. I can't believe how fast it's rising."

The water was cold. Very cold. And higher than my waist.

"Are you okay?" I asked. "What happened?"

"My foot is caught under a piece of concrete," she

said. "I had just noticed the water on the floor and was turning to get out of here. But the roof fell in. I tried to jump back, but I wasn't quick enough."

"Hang on," I said. "I'm going under to check things out."

I sucked in a deep breath and closed my eyes. I ducked beneath the water. As it bubbled around my head, I reached out until my hand bumped into Lisa's knee. I followed her leg downward to her foot.

Then I felt the chunk of concrete that had her trapped.

I got a good hold on the concrete block with both hands.

I tugged.

Nothing happened.

I tugged again.

Still nothing.

I was running out of air.

I tried one last time.

I couldn't move it at all. Because I was floating in the water, when I pulled, all I did was pull myself closer to the chunk of concrete.

No air left.

I stood up. When I broke free of the water, I gasped.

"I can't move it," I said.

She wrapped her arms around one of mine. "I'm so afraid," she said.

"Me too," I admitted.

"This is my fault," she blurted. "All because I hated Joey. I didn't mean for him to get hurt. I just wanted him out of *our* paintball game. I wanted him to look stupid for getting caught right away."

"You told the warriors ahead of time where he would be, didn't you?" I asked. "It had to be you. You and Micky made the plans the night before. Only you and Micky knew where Joey would be hiding."

"I didn't want him to be part of the Sewer Rats," she said.

"Because of your dad, right?" I asked. "Because he's Joey's stepdad."

"When Dad and Mom split up, Dad moved out of town," Lisa said. "Then he got married again. His new wife already had two kids. Joey was one of them. And they just moved back to town. It isn't fair that Joey gets my dad when I want so much for him to be with Mom and me."

She started to cry.

"Why did Joey want to join the Sewer Rats?" I asked. "I mean, he must have known it would make you mad."

"The first day he was at school, he thought we should try to be friends," Lisa said. "So he asked if he could hang with us. I told him he was stupid and I hated him and that he wasn't cool enough. Then he got mad and said he would join the Sewer Rats just to bug me. And all the time he pretended like he wasn't mad, like he just wanted to be friends, because it made me look bad."

That explained why she had made him do the test at the duck ponds instead of just trying him out in a

106

paintball game. And why he didn't let it show that anything she did bothered him. I wondered what I would have done in his place. He really seemed like a pretty good guy.

"Jimmy?"

"Yes?"

"The water. Pretty soon it's going to . . ."

"Don't say it," I said. It was almost up to my chest. She was a little taller than me, but it would be getting high on her too. "Worrying won't help."

"It's not about worrying," she said. "I wanted to tell you that maybe you should go."

"What?!"

"The water is rising so fast, I don't think Micky will be able to get help in time," she said. "You shouldn't have to stay with me. There's no reason for both of us to drown."

The water was nearly up to my armpits. I couldn't imagine how horrible it would be for Lisa. First it would reach her mouth. Then her nose.

She began to cry. "I'm scared," she said. "I don't want to die."

I couldn't leave her.

But would I let myself drown with her?

Under the water, I held her hand.

"I'm afraid too."

"I don't want to die," she said. "I don't want to die."

All I had to do was reach up. I could crawl back over the wall and save myself.

"Jimmy," she said, almost sobbing. "Do you think

there's a God and a heaven and angels and a place for me to be happy?"

I knew why she was asking. Thinking about dying is scary.

"Yes," I said. "I believe there is."

She held my hand tighter.

"Jimmy, don't leave me." She stopped and took a deep shaky breath. "You have to go. You have to save yourself."

I didn't know what to do. Staying with her wouldn't help. But how could I leave? But if I didn't leave, I'd drown too.

I realized I was glad that I wasn't as worried about dying as I thought I might be. I really did believe there was a place and Someone waiting for me.

Then something hit my head—a hand from above.

"Jim? Lisa? You guys okay?"

It was Micky's voice. And Micky's hand. He was coming through the opening over the cave-in.

I grabbed Micky's hand and pulled.

Twenty-Three

Micky landed beside us with a splash.

I was shaking with cold. I was already on my tiptoes. The water had to be close to Lisa's shoulders by now.

"I got up to the street through the manhole," Micky said as he struggled to his feet. "I sent someone to get help. But I had to come back."

"We're in trouble," I told him. "I don't think we have too much time left. And I can't get Lisa's foot loose."

I explained about the concrete block that had her trapped.

"How about this," he said. "Jim, we'll both go under. With the two of us, we can probably lift that block."

"I don't care if you rip my foot off," Lisa said. "Do what it takes."

"All right," I said. "Micky, don't think I'm weird. But we better hold hands when we go under. Trust me, we'll be working blind."

He grabbed my hand. We both ducked under the water and followed Lisa's leg down to the concrete block.

Everything seemed to move in slow motion as we swirled around. Gurgling sounds filled my ears. I kept my eyes squeezed shut. Micky and I both got our hands around the concrete.

Then we pulled.

Nothing.

We pulled again.

No movement.

I couldn't hold my breath any longer. I popped back to the surface. But I couldn't stand and keep my mouth above water.

I paddled.

"Jim!" Lisa cried. "The water's up to my neck!"

Micky came up, panting for air.

"We've got to get her out of here!" I shouted.

"Okay. Let's try again," Micky said. "But this time, when you get a good hold, pull yourself down into a squat. Plant your feet and lift, like you're trying to stand with it. Use your leg muscles. Got it? Even if we break our backs, we don't stop lifting. And Lisa, if you feel *anything* move, yank your foot free."

We didn't give her a chance to answer.

Micky grabbed my hand and we went down into the water again.

I reached for the chunk of concrete and got a good grip with both hands. I felt Micky's hands beside mine. I bumped against him as we both went into squats.

We tried to stand, straining against the weight. The rough edges of the concrete tore the skin off my fingers. Still, I pulled. A grunt left my mouth and bubbled air into the water.

Just a little, the concrete shifted.

I strained harder. Micky must have done the same. Because I felt more movement.

But I couldn't try again. I needed air. I pushed off and popped up beside Lisa. Micky splashed up beside me, gasping for air.

"I'm free!" Lisa shouted into the darkness. "Let's get out of here!"

Micky and I yelled with joy. If we could have seen each other, we would have been high-fiving like dancing fools.

Micky pushed Lisa toward the top of the wall. He followed close behind her, and I was right on his heels.

Getting out was easier than getting in. Our wet clothes made the dirt slick and slippery. And this time, I wasn't scared of getting stuck.

There was only one problem. The wall was beginning to break apart beneath us.

I didn't know that until Lisa and Micky helped me down on the other side. I landed on the tunnel floor with a splash in a small stream of water.

In the dim light from the open manhole cover, we could see the water flowing out of a crack in the wall. We knew how much water the wall held back, waiting to explode on us if the wall gave way.

"We've got to run," I said. "If this wall goes, we're in big trouble."

We took off for the main tunnel and the ladder to the manhole as fast as we could in the dim light.

We heard a low rumble as we reached the ladder.

"If the wall breaks," Micky shouted, "hook your arms through the rungs so the water doesn't take you away."

Micky and I pushed Lisa onto the ladder. She began to frantically pull herself up.

The rumble became thunder.

Micky and I both grabbed the ladder as Lisa rose.

The thunder of water became a roar.

"Climb! Climb!" I shouted.

Micky had climbed a quarter of the way up when the wall of water hit. I held on to the ladder just below him.

I hooked both of my arms between the iron rungs. The water slammed into me. If I hadn't gotten such a good hold, it would have swept me away.

The water pulled at my hair and my clothes. I still clung to the ladder though. All I had to do was hold my breath.

Then boom, something hit me in the leg. It felt like it had the force of a train. My last thought was short and simple. I couldn't believe the heat of the pain of a broken bone.

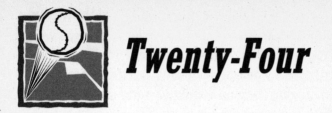

Twenty-Four

Miss Winkle, you know the rest of it.

When the surge of water got past us, the three of us were still hanging on the ladder. Soaked, cold, but alive.

But if Micky hadn't told me to hook my arms through the ladder, I might not be. Because I was unconscious. Later, the doctors decided that a big piece of concrete must have hit my leg. They guessed the water—and the concrete—was doing close to thirty miles an hour. Enough to break the bone.

I woke up screaming as the paramedics were loading me into an ambulance.

And, Miss Winkle, that's about the end of the story.

Unless you count what happened when I finally got out of the hospital, when I sat on the sidelines a couple of weeks later and watched the rest of the team play the Medford jerks again.

The game really didn't matter to us in terms of

standings. We were in last place and with only two games left in the season, it didn't look like we would move up even a single position.

This game meant something to the Medford jerks though. It was their last game in the season. If they won, they would become the first team ever in the league to go an entire season without losing a single game.

By the way they strutted onto the field, it looked like they were already planning their victory celebration.

As I watched from the bleachers, my leg in a cast, my hands began to hurt. I looked down and saw that I was gripping the bleachers so hard that my knuckles and the backs of my hands were white from lack of blood.

I guess I wanted our team to win.

We had first at bat. Their pitcher, Murphy Kay, was a gangly guy with a big nose and a pimple almost as big in the center of his forehead. He was all arms and legs in his windup, and by the time the ball left his fingers, it looked like his hand was almost at the plate.

He was good, and he knew it. But our team was hungry. Joey had become friends with most of us, and we remembered what they had done to him.

Micky started the inning by lining a single up the middle. Lisa, up next, got under the ball. Her short looper hit the ground between the first baseman and the right fielder. So we had two runners on base with none out. Pimple Head struck out the next two batters. Rainbow, however, took a wild swing at a wild pitch and got lucky, smashing a shot past the third baseman for a single into left field. Micky scored, and Lisa pulled up at third. Our next batter struck out, leaving two runners on.

One to nothing, Tigers.

Micky put on a great show in his first inning on the mound.

He began by facing one of their best hitters, the military leader with the name Barksdale across the back of his perfectly clean jersey. Micky decided to play a little chin music for the guy, throwing it high and inside. Barksdale jerked back as if someone had tied a rope around his neck and taken off running. He backed out of the box but made a big deal about digging right in again. The fans, most of them here for Medford, booed loudly.

Micky winked at me and threw another blistering pitch, this one even closer to the guy's chin. It rattled Barksdale so badly that he went down swinging at air on the next three pitches.

After that, Micky decided to play nice. He had a curveball that snapped inside at the end, and he used it and fastballs to keep their hitters off balance.

Three batters, three strikeouts.

And that was only the beginning.

Pimple Head got through the next four innings without letting a single one of the Tigers hit out of the infield.

But Micky did the same.

The sixth inning began with us still leading 1–0.

Lisa led off with a perfect bunt down the left line. Their third baseman decided to see if it would roll foul. But it didn't. Lisa made it safely to first.

Then she stole second on a wild pitch.

Rainbow hit her home.

Two to nothing, Tigers lead.

Joey stood beside me. Our voices sounded hoarse from yelling and cheering. It was the bottom of the ninth, and we'd scored two more times, but they'd scored twice too. Four to two.

Micky walked the first batter he faced. And the second. Everyone could see that he was getting tired. But we didn't have another good pitcher. We were still a pretty ragtag team.

So Micky just gritted his teeth and kept throwing. Their third batter hit a ball solid, just foul. On the next pitch, he lined one toward second, right at Lisa's head. She caught it, came down, and tried to tag the runner but missed.

One down, runners still at first and second.

Micky's curve had lost its snap, and his fastball no longer came in on a straight rope. Their fourth batter fouled off the first couple of pitches, and Micky was grunting with effort. Finally, Micky found an inside corner on a pitch their batter just watched. Strike three.

Two down, runners still at first and second.

Micky was so tired, he walked the next batter.

Two down, bases loaded. The Tigers were only up by two runs. A double would tie the game. A triple or home run would beat us.

And Barksdale was their next batter. He grinned his cocky grin.

His first swing fouled off the tip of his bat, and the ball disappeared into the stands. His second swing did the same. Two strikes, no balls.

Later, Micky told me he threw his next pitch out of sheer desperation. Micky knew that if he tried a fastball, Barksdale would just ride it out of the park.

So Micky tossed an underhand pitch.

Underhand. Like a softball pitch.

It came in high and slow. Barksdale must have had about ten seconds to decide how to hit it. It was too much time. He took a giant cut, trying to send it out of the park. He missed!

Coming around with the bat almost screwed him into the ground.

All the Tigers headed to the mound to congratulate Micky. He ran from them, though, and led them all to where I was sitting and yelling. For the next few minutes, the sky disappeared above me as bodies and noise surrounded me.

Twenty-Five

When everyone had left at the end of the game, Micky came back over to me with his backpack. He dug into it and pulled out an armful of comics.

"Thought you might like these," he said. He tossed them onto my lap. "With that cast, you're not going anywhere for a while."

He sat on the bench beside me.

For a few minutes, we didn't talk. Parents drove away from the field with the Medford players. Coach Martin was waiting in the parking lot near his van, but he didn't come over to tell us to hurry. He had offered to take me home since my parents were busy with my brother and sisters.

"I've got to ask you," I finally said to Micky. "In the sewer, why did you come back? Don't get me wrong. If it wasn't for you, we would have never gotten Lisa loose. But from what you've said about your dad, and him going into the burning car, and how you think heroes are stupid . . ."

I held my breath. I didn't want Micky to get mad and leave.

Micky surprised me. He grinned.

"I've been thinking about that," he said. "A lot."

He took a deep breath.

"Why did I go back? It's like this. I couldn't not do it. Does that make sense?"

I thought about why I'd kept trying to help Lisa. I nodded my head to show him I understood.

"And I've been thinking more," he said. "About my dad."

I waited.

"All along I've been mad at him because I thought he was trying to be a hero," Micky said. "But now I don't think it was like that. For him, it was probably the same as for us. We couldn't stand by and watch. We had to do something. Or we'd hate ourselves for standing by."

I nodded some more. I'd learned brave wasn't about not having fear. It was about allowing yourself to be afraid. And not quitting because of that fear.

"You know what the newspapers said about us," Micky said. He made a face and shook his head. "But we're not heroes. It's just that other people have decided to call us that."

Micky looked at his hands and thought for a few more seconds.

"Anyway," he said. "For a long time I've been angry at my dad because I thought he died trying to be a hero. I hated him. I mean, I thought he cared so little about me and Mom that he threw away his life just for the chance to become a hero."

Micky smiled sadly. "I guess I know different now, don't I?"

"Yeah," I said. "I guess so."

Micky's smile grew less sad. "So I don't hate him anymore. In a way, it's like having him back—which is pretty cool after all these years."

That was all Micky said. Then he helped me to Coach Martin's van.

When I got home, I unloaded the comic books Micky had given me. I noticed the one on top. It was about a galactic soldier who never lost his battles against evil aliens.

I tossed the comic book under my bed. I wasn't that interested.

In a way, Micky had his father back.

Me? I didn't need Zantor anymore.